THAT DOG
WON'T
HUNT

THAT DOG WON'T HUNT

LOU ALLIN

RAVEN BOOKS
an imprint of
ORCA BOOK PUBLISHERS

Library and Archives Canada Cataloguing in Publication

Allin, Lou, 1945-
That dog won't hunt / written by Lou Allin.
(Rapid reads)

Issued also in an electronic format.
ISBN 978-1-55469-339-9

I. Title. II. Series: Rapid reads
PS8551.L5564T43 2010   C813'.6   C2010-903657-3

First published in the United States, 2010
Library of Congress Control Number: 2010929176

Summary: A drifter takes a job at a hunting lodge in
Northern Ontario, with the expectation of a big payday for
the summer's work. But when the eccentric owner decides
to renege on her promises, she ends up dead. (RL 2.8)

Mixed Sources
Cert no. SW-COC-001271
© 1996 FSC
FSC

*Orca Book Publishers is dedicated to preserving the environment and has
printed this book on paper certified by the Forest Stewardship Council.*

Orca Book Publishers gratefully acknowledges the support for
its publishing programs provided by the following agencies: the
Government of Canada through the Canada Book Fund and the
Canada Council for the Arts, and the Province of British Columbia
through the BC Arts Council and the Book Publishing Tax Credit.

Design by Teresa Bubela
Cover photography by Getty Images

ORCA BOOK PUBLISHERS
PO Box 5626, Stn. B
Victoria, BC Canada
V8R 6S4

ORCA BOOK PUBLISHERS
PO Box 468
Custer, WA USA
98240-0468

www.orcabook.com
Printed and bound in Canada.

13 12 11 10 • 4 3 2 1
699749

To all the dogs that have enriched my life:
Pebbles, Freya, Nikon, Friday, Shogun, Zia...
and Bucky.

CHAPTER ONE

This mirage was made to order. A cherry-red Mustang Mach 1 sat by the side of the road in the Mojave Desert. Its hood was up. Waves of heat rolled off the asphalt like X-rays.

My eyes were sore from squinting. One side of my throat was tickling the other. I took the last swig from a plastic gallon of water I'd bought at Twentynine Palms. Scored a three-pointer against a saguaro. The jug rolled like a tumble-weed. I had been hitching on I-10 east from LA. They might be looking for me on the Interstate, so I took this back road through the Sheephole Mountains toward Vegas. Hadn't seen one damn car in an hour.

Cowboy boots hate asphalt and sand. Fact is, they're not big on walking, period. I hoisted my duffel over my shoulder and headed for the car. The sun beat down like honey. Too dry in the desert for sweat to even bead. Thank god it was April, not July.

"Damn it to hell!" a rough voice yelled. The rear plate read *Ontario*. My mirage was near perfect. Canucks are helpful, and they'll swallow hard-luck stories. Then the hood slammed down.

A wiry woman, barely five feet, with a wide straw hat and sunglasses, puffed on a cigarillo. Female. Three for three. Leading with my "trust me" grin, I approached.

"Where did you come from, cowboy?" she asked, tapping the ash and smiling with a plump red mouth. My boyish look makes women want to mother me.

"A lady in distress?" I took a mock bow, sweeping off my hat. It was battered and stained from a beating I'd rather forget.

Why was she out here alone? Where was she heading? Surely as far as Utah. Canada was way past that.

"You look like a man who knows horses. How about Mustangs?"

Smiling, I trailed a finger over the dust on the door. Hand-buffed and detailed. Someone loved it.

"Let's take a look." Raising the matte black hood with that sexy scoop, I fixed the safety rod.

She took off the hat and fanned herself. The cat's-eye sunglasses made her look like Cher. Throaty laughter said hard years of liquor and tobacco.

"It's fate. Looks like we both took the wrong road. Nothing's come along but a couple of vultures ready to pick my bones." She pointed to a circling bird.

"Shame to waste such pretty bones. Anyways, it's a red hawk. You can tell by the whistle." I reached in and turned the key to watch the gauges. "Not outta gas. Oil's good. Not overheating. What happened to her?"

She shrugged and flipped the plastic tip of the cigarillo toward the sagebrush. "Got herky-jerky at first. Nearly slowed to a stop." She wore a white linen skirt and a floral blouse. Silk scarf around her neck. Like she'd come from a business meeting. Not many women could keep their cool alone in the desert.

I tossed an appreciative glance just to let her know I noticed.

"One thing's sure, we gotta get out of here. Start her up." I moved to the front.

The engine caught right off. But instead of a purr, she sounded like she had the hiccups. Not in the starter then. No backfiring or pinging either. Dirty fuel line?

I signaled to turn off the ignition. Spark-plug connections were good, carburetor flap moved easy. When I removed the distributor cap, I knew what was wrong.

"More gas. But nice and easy. She's talking."

Give Daddy a paper clip, a screwdriver, duct tape and a hose and he'd get anything with wheels moving. From my jeans pocket, I pulled a penknife with a bone handle. Then I exposed the points and scraped.

"Try her now." Listening, I held up a hand, and she read me loud and clear. The engine stopped. I scraped again. "She's hurting but back in business."

The Mustang had enough life to get us to a town. The woman revved the motor.

"You're one damn miracle worker. I'd like to shake your hand, kind sir."

I took out my last handkerchief and cleaned my fingers. "Glad to help."

"I'm Gladys Ryan." She had a firm grip, like she knew what she was doing. It's a western thing. I'm all for being equal. Some women I've seen could ride and rope circles around me. Credit where credit's due, and all that. She wore a real strange ring on her third finger, left hand. Like a cigar band, only colored metal.

"Rick Cooper."

"Gary Cooper. Tall, dark and handsome."

"No relation, ma'am." Mama used to like that dude. Another good sign.

"Looks like we both caught a break. Hop in. You drive," she said.

I tossed my duffel into the trunk beside her set of fancy luggage marked *YSL*. Maybe it was secondhand. Then I eased into the seat and took the leather-wrapped wheel. Daddy always said to keep your hands at ten and two. Looking at the gearshift, I did a double take.

"What the hell's that?"

She gave a little pound to the dash as she laughed. "That's the future, if you get old enough. A steel hip joint."

"I've seen custom, but this beats all." I found first and juiced the gas. I went through all five gears, double-clutching at the top to show off.

Some fierce stink filled the car. "Oh, Christ. Bucky's awake."

"Huh?" I hadn't seen a kid. She was a bit old for that.

"It's my golden retriever in the backseat. You'd never know he was there unless he wakes up for a meal. Then he farts up a storm."

Turns out Bucky was fifteen, old for the breed and on the deaf side. She and her husband had him from a pup. Retrievers weren't my thing. Didn't see the point of them. German shepherds, maybe. Good guard dogs earned their keep.

Her tiny hand reached out to adjust the air conditioner. Blue veins. Not so young then.

Maybe a rough fifty or a prime sixty. That could work in my favor.

"The gearshift was my late husband George's. He had a hip replacement and a wicked sense of humor."

"Uh-huh." That explained the weird ring. Must've been a cheap bastard.

"I do admire the car. She's choice." Fifty thousand miles on the odometer. Babied big-time for twenty years. "No rust neither. Saw your license. Don't you have salt on the road up there?"

"Kept it covered up inside all winter. Too light in the rear for traction. We used it only for special trips. George had a sister in San Diego. We went down once a year." Her voice took on a sad tone. "I'm... coming back from her funeral."

"Sorry for your loss."

She shrugged and pooched out her lower lip. "She was eighty. When you gotta go..."

"It's not bad to go in California."

"You got that right. How'd you know that trick with the engine?" She reached into the backseat.

"My daddy purely loved Mustangs. The '65 classic, and then the '70 like this one: 351 Cleveland V-8 engine. Same color too. Christmas cars, he called 'em. Red, green, gold stripes." I heard her rummaging around. A metallic clinking. My lips were chapped and I licked them. "Sure would be funny if it was the same one," I said.

"In the movies maybe. George bought this new. Five thousand bucks." She popped the cap off a can of Colt 45 and passed it over.

"That'll hit the spot. Lots of snow up north?" I finished the brew in a couple of gulps.

"We don't all live in igloos like Yanks think. But we plow and shovel plenty of the white stuff." Next came a paper cup and a bottle of Smirnoff. She poured herself a generous slug and toasted me.

CHAPTER TWO

At a constant ninety mph, we were eating up that desert. At Amboy, we turned east toward Needles. "I've heard of Toronto. They have the Blue Jays."

"Wimps in the Banana Belt. Now, you take Wawa."

"Wa...huh?"

"It's a town in Northern Ontario where they have a big goose."

"For real?"

"A tourist attraction statue, silly boy. People make jokes about going up by Wawa. Then back by choo choo."

The joke was lame, but I laughed. Maybe she'd spring for dinner. One thing for sure: that car would take a day or two to fix. Getting twenty-year-old parts wouldn't be easy.

She gave my arm a friendly punch. "So tell me about yourself, Rick. We've got some road to cover. You look like the real thing, not some rhinestone cowboy like the song."

The leather seat was cooling off. I breathed deeply and settled back like I owned the world. She listened, not like a lot of girls I'd met.

I told her how I grew up in a double-wide in Escalante, Utah. Tires on the top to keep the roof on. Daddy was a heavy-equipment mechanic for a local mine until it shut down. Same year Mama died from a snakebite. She had been planting flowers by the house. Just wanted a little color. I was only ten.

"That must have been hard. A boy needs his mother." She patted my shoulder. "Go on."

I said that a couple of weeks later, Daddy gave me a hug and put the bone-handled knife in my hand. "I called your Uncle Seth in Salt Lake. He'll come get you. You're okay, kid, but I'm not cut out to be a father. Maybe you will be. It's an important job. Never forget that." I waved as that Mustang headed down the road. Children's Aid came instead of Uncle Seth. Foster homes. Back of the hand or a leather belt for any smart talk. I quit school at sixteen and went to work on a ranch. But I was always looking for Daddy to come around that curve. Christ, he was probably dead now.

I found myself opening up like a cactus flower. Something wet touched my eye. I hadn't never told no one about all this. Thirty years old and I felt like a kid again. Gladys had the bottle half gone. When I crushed the empty can I'd been holding, she passed me another brew.

"Last one for now. You're driving. By the way, I'm going to Vegas. That suit you?" Her words were losing their edge.

No one would be looking for me in a cherry Mustang. Once in Vegas, truckers headed for Salt Lake could take me across to Utah.

"Perfect."

"So what's a nice country boy like you doing out in the middle of nowhere?" she asked, as the vodka bottle clinked at her feet. "You sound like you're fresh off the ranch."

"Guess you might say I'm seeing the world." I didn't add that when my last wrangling job ended, I took a bus to LA with a buddy. Got in deeper than I reckoned, looking for some fast money. The coke shipment I was sent to deliver got stolen on the way. A couple of homeboys with guns left me in a vacant lot with a killer lump on my head. I was pretty sure the guys I was working for wouldn't appreciate losing forty thousand. But I didn't wait around to find out.

She looked over at me and her eyelids fluttered. "I'm a good judge of character. Sort of a sixth sense."

We were on Route 40, a mile from Needles. The sooner we were away from cities, the better. In the wide-open spaces, you could see who was coming.

People were funny about drugs. Especially her age group. I took a silent breath and tried to sound casual. "I've worked on a few ranches. Thought California might be my style. The San Joaquin Valley has lots of farms. Fruit and nuts mainly. I was getting good at repairing equipment. Then the economy tanked. Back in Utah I can always get stock work. Doesn't pay much, but it's steady."

"Leave a woman behind?" she asked.

"No, but I left a good horse. Nufflo's running pasture at a friend's."

From the center of Needles, I took Route 95 north.

The desert flew by as we crossed into Nevada. I held the wheel loose and easy but ready for action. Like the reins on Nufflo. He was my bud. We'd seen some times together out on the range.

"What's your dream, Gary? You're a young man."

I didn't bother to correct her about my name. But what a funny question. No one had ever asked me that. And I had to think a bit before opening my yap.

"Oh, a few acres between Church Wells and Big Water outside Escalante. Not far from the Arizona border. Nothing special. A cabin and enough room for a horse." I was through with big plans. Being greedy was plain stupid.

"Wells and water. Sounds like the desert all right. Bet there's not a mosquito in miles."

"In the canyons around the seeps or the potholes after a gully washer maybe. Watching the sun go down behind the Coxcomb is the prettiest sight in the world. Doesn't cost nothing."

"The Coxcomb. Very romantic names out west. Small dreams can be good dreams."

She took off her dark glasses and looked at me, and I nearly drove off the road. Her eyes were like blue ice at the bottom of a glacier. They bore clean into me and out the back. One wheel hit the sand. The rear end twisted, but I held on.

"Sorry," I said. Some women would have screamed. She was real calm.

"You're looking at my eyes. Everyone does. They're not contacts. Just Burns eyes." They ran in her family. Clear back to Finland or somewhere. She was talking

17

slower and slower. Like she was winding down.

"Mom had a border collie once with one eye blue, the other brown. Like he had two sides to him," I said.

"Devil and angel." We both started to laugh. "I'm a little of both too. And I won't forget that I owe you." Her head turned toward the window.

She was quiet for a few minutes. I didn't have much else to say, so I drove in silence. Close enough for a signal now. I fiddled with the radio.

"So what kind of mu…"

But she was snoring. Her hat had come off. The black hair was a dye job, dark as a raven. Good skin though. Babied like the car. Deep blue eye shadow. Fragile lids. You could see where her makeup ended above her neck. Poor old bat. Where did she get off picking up a guy in the desert? Someone could take her for everything she had.

Leave her out there and drive off. What the hell. Soon we'd be in Vegas. Maybe I'd get a meal and a few bucks. Even bus fare. She did say she owed me.

Phil Collins was singing "Another Day in Paradise."

The highway stretched ahead, and the gas gauge was sinking. We weren't far from Henderson. Watching the moon and reading casino billboards had been keeping me awake. The desert was prettier plain. I saw a rattler making its way across the highway and aimed for it. Looked like a stick, but I knew better. Big sucker. Seven feet at least. In the rear-view mirror, it whipped back and forth. Nobody home but still moving. Dead rattlers bite more people than live ones. I don't blame them. It's their nature.

"Score one for Mama," I whispered.

I pulled over at the town limits. Just in time. I was getting sleepy. No sense in us getting into a wreck. Where did she want me to take her? I touched her arm gently. "Hey, wake up, ma'am." The vodka fumes hit me, and she rolled toward the window. My stomach was emptier than a hollow gourd. About as loud too.

Her big leather purse was on the floor. I picked it up. Hairbrush. Compact. Woman stuff. A huge wad of bills, wrapped with an elastic, nestled in my hand. A fake roll? Leafing, I saw hundreds winking at me. "Wheew," I whistled softly. My palm began to itch. Not enough for the ranch though. Why had I told her about it? Somewhere, a siren filled the air.

They'd pick me off like a lizard on a wall. I was no gambling man, but I'd play this hand straight up. I drove ahead. Neon lights announced motels. More expensive as the road reached the center of town with the big hotels. Gladys was still dead out. I had to make a decision.

The Wild West Motel was clean but not fancy. After paying with one of the hundreds, I asked for a quiet room at the back. I parked, then collected Gladys. She was light as a yearling. Her face looked trusting, peaceful. I placed her on one of the beds. Took off her shoes and scarf. Pulled a light blanket over her. She'd have a humdinger of a hangover the next morning—or maybe not.

Damn few women can finish nearly a whole bottle. It was a miracle she was still alive, but something told me she was used to this. I went back for what Mama called an overnight case. So's she could freshen up in the morning. I let the dumbass dog out for a pee and a dump, then left the car windows down for him.

Back inside, I tested the other bed. Hard, but better than the car. Cheap TV, commercial carpet with a few scorches, a desk and chest of drawers. Never many lights. Guess people don't want to see too clear in places like this. On the wall was a big ship with a hundred sails. I never wanted to go to sea. The desert was my ocean. Miles and miles and miles of space. One of my teachers said it was all water once. What a crazy idea.

The smell rising off me was almost as bad as the stale tobacco and mold in the air. I took a long, hot shower and gave myself a quick shave with the little soap. I checked my pockets for change and went down the hall to the machine. Wouldn't be the first time I had a Snickers bar and bag of Fritos for dinner.

Back in the room, I pulled the drapes and stripped to my underwear. Then I lay down on the other double bed, finishing eating in record time. I fell asleep to the sound of Gladys burbling along with the swamp cooler. I was dreaming about my old cowpony Nufflo. Was he still watching for me?

Something woke me in the middle of the night.

CHAPTER THREE

C ar tires screeched outside. A jet took off. Then an eighteen-wheeler's motor gunned. A strong sun lit the corners of the drapes. I struggled to open my gritty eyes. Gladys was sitting in a lacy black slip on the only chair, blowing smoke rings. Three, four, five.

"Morning, sunshine," she said.

If I hadn't seen that empty bottle, I would've thought I'd dreamed it. The dog was sleeping on the floor, an ice bucket filled with water next to him.

"Morning, yourself." I let a smile do the talking. Maybe she didn't even remember what happened last night. "Coffee? Know I could do with some. Back in a flash."

She nodded. Somehow she had fixed herself: hair, clothes and makeup. The old girl had powers.

"Know what? You're a handy man."

I pulled on my jeans and last clean shirt, then boots.

"There's a restaurant down the way. Bunch of trucks outside last night. A good sign."

"Usually is." She was tapping ashes into a fake potted plant. "Just coffee for now. I take mine black. And strong."

Fifteen minutes later, I brought back a couple of donuts with the large coffees. "Cinnamon. My favorite," she said. "Aren't you the mind reader?"

Her teeth were her own. Little, sharp and white.

25

I took a seat on the bed while she opened the cup, inhaling the aroma.

"Damn. I forgot. We need to get the car to a garage."

"Arranged for that next door," I said. "She'll be ready tomorrow. New plugs, new points. Water pump's on the fritz too. Special order from the junkyard. Save you a bit that way."

"Well done then." Gladys arched one eyebrow and crossed her legs. "I guess we're loose on the town. Right time at the right place. You a gambling man?"

"No way. I got ten bucks and it's gotta get me home." I took out my wallet and showed her the lone bill.

"You could have had more. And you know it."

She looked at me with those ice-diamond eyes again. I could feel them undressing me. Like they did in the dark last night. I might never walk straight again.

Who knew that an old lady had that much energy?

"Let's hit the quarter slots. More fun than profit. Then a big dinner's in order. My treat. You don't have anyplace you have to be, do you?"

I thought of the long road ahead. Back to work for me. It might take years to earn the money for that small ranch.

"I'm all yours." I tossed her a wink. Her face brightened, and I wondered how far I could go.

Casinos know the bottom line. Only big spenders get free drinks. I hustled us a few beers. Gladys gambled down to her last quarter, then hit a jackpot that paid five hundred.

"Gotta know when to fold 'em," she said, loading her stash into the plastic buckets. At the wicket she traded her coins for twenties. Outside, we blinked in the light. Night was better here. In the dark,

27

it was all one big cozy bear den in the middle of nowhere, its own country with no clocks.

"Come on," Gladys said, taking my arm. "I remember a good spot from the old days."

At the Branding Iron Restaurant, we ordered up two T-bones, baked potatoes, salad bar. Pitcher of Bud.

"Beer is an honest drink," she said. "Order wine in any of these places, the markup is three hundred percent."

Gladys ate everything on her plate, even the green stuff. Must have had a metabolism like a jackrabbit. She took out her cigarillos.

"I didn't forget last night," she said. "That was a treat."

"Not sure what you mean, ma'am," I said, tucking the last piece of steak into my mouth. Mama lived long enough to teach me manners. "Pleasure's all mine."

"You know full well, cowboy. And stop it with the ma'ams. You're making me feel old." She finished the glass of beer and wiped her mouth carefully. "You got any real plans? Anything that can't wait?"

I shrugged. She was getting at something. "I like working with my hands. Never get rich that way, but it's enough."

"Your hands are far from ordinary." She sat back and worked her lips over a thought. "What skills do you have?"

"Little of everything. Carpentry. Electrical. Plumbing. When you work on a ranch, there's always something needs fixing. I pay attention. Experience is way better than books."

"Smart man." She observed me like a prime steer. There was hunger in those cool eyes. Like dry ice smoldering. "I have a proposition."

Gladys and her late husband George owned a hunting lodge a few hours north of Sault Ste. Marie in Northern Ontario. Several hundred acres with wilderness up the wazoo. They took tourists on bear and moose hunts at over two grand a week, meals and rooms included. He had passed with a heart attack five years ago.

"I'll be honest with you, Rick. He was a lot older than me. The father I never had, and my best friend too. I miss him, but life goes on. It's taken me a while to realize that. Everything's gone to pot."

"What do you mean?" She seemed to be doing all right. Car, clothes, cash.

"The climate's rough in Canada. Much can go wrong in a few years. The maintenance is brutal."

"What's its name, your lodge?" I asked. Things were falling into place. Sounded as good as a big ranch.

"Call of the Wild. Americans are suckers for that stuff. Especially from the big eastern cities. Imagine charging folks to stay in the bush. Why, we just got electricity in. Before that it was lanterns and hand pumps."

"Here they call 'em dude ranches," I said with a nod. "Same difference."

"Look...Rick," she said. "We can do each other a favor. You need a job, right? I need a man."

I didn't answer. Pop always said, "Keep your mouth shut, no one knows you're a fool. Open it, and they're sure."

"This is a business proposal. Not that I didn't appreciate the...other service," she said, patting my hand. "There's plenty for both of us."

"How long are we talking?"

"You'll be home on the range before Christmas. Count on it. And your share will be a fair one."

"What would that be? Just asking." I spoke with respect because I didn't want to blow my chances.

"Oh...four hundred a week, give or take. But that's chicken feed. We'll settle up the big money at the end."

"Sounds okay then. So we're all set?"

She folded her arms, tanned and wiry. Not like most sixty-year-old women.

"We need a way to get you over the border. There's no time for an official work permit. And I don't want my escort to look like a tramp. No offense." Then she called the waiter over and ordered a raw sirloin to go for Bucky.

The first stop was a clothes store. Gladys flashed her Visa until it was smoking. Pants, shirts, jeans, jackets. I picked up a hundred-dollar Stetson, but she shook her head. "Too damn cold where you're going. You'll need something with ear flaps."

I held up a jim-dandy pair of alligator boots. Everyone knew Tony Lama.

"Not this time, bub. Those high heels get stuck in muskeg, you're a goner. Let's go with some work boots."

At a barbershop, she got me a haircut and the closest shave I ever had.

"Follow my lead. If we play it straight, we'll have no problem at the border. After all, what do we have to hide?" she asked, touching my cheek and sniffing the after-shave. "Old Spice. George used to wear that."

CHAPTER FOUR

Over the next couple of days, we made our way east, then north. I felt kind of sad driving through Utah without stopping. Not many folks appreciate this rough country. Dad said it was the last part of the US ever mapped. Gladys just grunted at the Book Cliffs.

"Nice if you like rocks," she said. "But it's one long sand dune with damn few places to drink. Look where we stopped for lunch in Green River. Dry counties. Supper clubs. That would never fly in Canada. We never even had Prohibition."

"Pro…what's that?"

"That's when alcohol was illegal. Back in the twenties. Even before my time."

"Liquor's hard to find in some counties. Mormons aren't supposed to drink. Where I live, they usually sneak down into Arizona to get their booze," I said.

Colorado was pretty but ritzy with all those ski resorts. We passed a bunch of big gas-sucking RVs slowed to nothing at the Eisenhower Tunnel. At Denver we joggled up to Nebraska. One big corn-field. We passed Des Moines and skirted Chicago. North of Lansing we took the I-75 north on a straight shot for Canada. That's when I started noticing the snow. Even in the desert we have a few inches at high elevations. This looked like the remains of twenty feet. It was collapsing on itself as it melted.

"Jesus," I said. "There's a million legs of dead deer sticking up."

Gladys laughed. "Happens every winter when they cross the highway. Plows shove the bodies to the berm. Life can be brutal if you're little...and weak."

At Sault Ste. Marie, Michigan, we slowed with the traffic. A sign said that we were heading for the same city in Canada. Go figure. Gladys freshened her lipstick in the mirror.

"Do just like I said, honey, and don't be nervous. We've known each other for years. Your father and George were army buddies. Hunted together. That's the way they think in Youperland. You're coming up for the summer to give me a hand. Which is true."

"Youperland?" I asked. Too many ideas flooded my head.

She sighed and shook her head.

"People who live in the Michigan Upper Peninsula are called Youpers. The U-P. Remember that big bridge?"

"Sure. This is one exam I'm going to ace," I said. They called me a slow learner or something until I quit in grade ten. Slow nothing. I had better things to do.

"They may have their suspicions, but there's not a damn thing they can do. Just imagine a tall, cool ice cube clear down to your toes. Slow your pulse. Think before each answer, but do it fast."

"You're the boss."

"One more thing. I might as well use up my limit."

We stopped at a hardware chain, and Gladys bought a Stihl. Biggest they had. When the clerk took it from the box, Gladys handed it to me.

"Here's your chainsaw, boy. When we get home, I want land cleared for more cabins."

Looks like she planned on getting her money's worth. So what? Hard work never killed no one.

"Okay, hon," I said.

After stopping a minute at the duty-free store, we crossed over into the Canadian Sault, and Gladys taught me the anthem as we started up the bridge.

"Coming south, George and I always used to sing it halfway to the flags, then the US anthem." She turned that ring on her finger, and I heard her sniff.

"I admire your ring. It's real unusual."

That brought a smile. "We didn't have a pot to pee in, starting out. George gave me a cigar band for a ring. Kind of a joke. Then he had this made. It's always been lucky for me. Remember, I had it on when I won that jackpot." She looked at it like an old friend. Maybe it was.

We headed for the booths. I pulled up to the window. She thought it would look better if I was driving. "Citizenship?" the officer asked.

"I'm American, and she's Canadian," I said. I showed a driver's license, and Gladys had her birth certificate.

"Anything to declare?"

"Just a chainsaw, duty-free liquor and cigarettes." Gladys handed over the slips. He glanced at them.

"You're a long way from home, sir. And the purpose of your trip?" the officer asked, emerging from his booth. He stepped forward and took a note of our plate.

"Just a visit for the summer," Gladys said.

The man's face was hard to read. Poker would have been his game. He gestured to a building. "You'll have to fill out a declaration form. Then see the immigration officer. Pull in over there and go up to the counter. Shouldn't take too long... unless you have warrants that show up on the computer."

Lou Allin

Inside, a fat female clerk gave us a number, and we took a seat on a wooden bench. My stomach turned over and rumbled. Gladys crossed her legs and sighed.

An hour later, she went into a small room with a table and two chairs. Twenty minutes had passed when she emerged, giving me an unseen nod. She was one smart lady. Then I entered the room as directed.

"Mr. Cooper, I understand you have known Mrs. Ryan for a number of years," the bald man said. *Haig* was on his name tag.

Like to have wiped that smirk off his face. I managed a decent blush instead. It had gotten me outta trouble more times than I can remember.

"Yes, sir. Daddy used to hunt with… Uncle George. Why, one time—"

"Never mind that." Haig tapped his pencil on the table. "How long are you going to be in Canada?"

Soon after, Gladys was brought into the room and we exchanged glances.

"Everything okay, officer?" she asked. "I simply don't understand why we're been disaccommodated. I have a mind to call my Member of Parliament. He was a friend of George's."

I smiled. Damn. She had one good vocabulary.

Haig looked like he had swallowed vinegar.

"You can go. But you must return to the US after two months, Mr. Cooper. Is that clear? If you wish to work in Canada or stay longer than that, you must apply for landed immigrant status."

"I understand. No problem."

Gladys moved out like she owned the place. I held the door for her.

On the way back to the car, I wanted to give a high five. But she motioned me to keep walking.

"'They can still see us. Smarten up."

I walked straight and cool, never even looking back.

Gladys opened the rye and poured herself a healthy snort. I popped a beer. The Soo, as she called it, looked like kind of a dump next to the US side, but I kept my mouth shut. Didn't want her to feel bad.

We stopped at a food store for some grocery basics. There would be nothing at the lodge but flour and a few canned goods.

"I could eat a horse. How about you?" Gladys asked. "Giovanni's makes great pasta. And I could use a bottle of their Chianti. You deserve a treat too. That guy must have put you through the wringer."

What did she mean about a ringer? They talked different up here.

"Yeah, kinda."

It was past dark when we left the grill after a couple of pounds of spaghetti and meatballs. I could have done with a nap after the drinks, but I could tell Gladdie wanted to get home. I'd taken to calling her that, and she seemed to like it. Bucky was let out but never seemed to have to go. He could last twelve hours between pit stops.

"Got no Interstates up here?" I asked. "Says Trans-Canada, but it's a two-lane cow path."

"Behave," she said. "Bigger isn't necessarily better." She muttered some directions.

An hour later we headed north around Elliot Lake. It was pitch-dark, but the snow cover on the ground and trees lightened things up. Pines, I guess, or spruce or fir. Reminded me of ponderosas but a hell of a lot smaller. The moon rising helped, and we passed swamp after swamp. Swamps meant mosquitoes. I had to use bug dope once when I went after trout at Fish Lake.

"Hope I haven't passed the place," I said to Gladys when she woke up. She lit a cigarette and the glow filled the cab.

43

Things all looked alike to me but not to her. "Another fifteen minutes," she said. "That's the old Royce cabin." She pointed at a burned-out shell. It was the first place I'd seen in thirty minutes.

"What the hell did they ever do up here?" I asked. "It's not ranching country."

She shrugged. "Farming is piss-poor except for hay and potatoes. Trappers opened up the country back in voyageur days."

"Like the hoser guys on TV? In plaid jackets? Back bacon?"

Gladys smothered a yawn. "Earlier than that. French Canadian explorers. Timber to follow. At Elliot Lake they had the uranium mine until that business went belly up."

"Your place doesn't glow none, does it?" I asked.

"It will now," she said. "You're going to make it sparkle." Then she sat up. "Slow down, sonnie. Next drive's ours," she said. She rummaged in her purse for a padlock key.

I got out and opened up. I removed the chain and pushed back the large gate. *Call of the Wild* was routered on a sign across the top. A mailbox stood by, barely on top of a snowbank. Someone had cleared the drive. Bucky woke up in the back and started barking.

"Home sweet home," Gladys said. "Harvey Freedman down the road has a contract to plow. He's been keeping her open all winter. Otherwise you'd need a backhoe." Suddenly returned to life, Bucky was pawing at the back window. She let him out and he started to run. It was the first time I'd seen him in any kind of action.

The house was a hundred yards through the forest. I heard a barred owl. "Who cooks for you?" the hoot asked. A good omen. I was looking forward to some rib-sticking meals. Living on fast food in California, I'd even dropped a couple of pounds.

We pulled to a stop in front of the main house, she called it. It was like a superbig A-frame with two stories and two large wings. A motion-sensor light went on. Gladys got out and put her hand on her back. "Oooo. Stiff." Then I heard a weird sound, like a mournful howl.

"Bucky's glad to be home," she said. "But he probably thinks George is still here. Dogs' minds work that way."

"I'll call Harvey to say we're back," she added. "Bring the bags in. Then start a fire. It's still damn cold here. Snow won't be gone for another week."

My breath hung in the air. "Okey dokey."

The ceilings were low in the hall. Gladys went around flicking on the lights. Everything was paneled in tongue-and-groove pine. It was a nice place but needed some TLC. Kind of like her.

The Great Room had huge windows reaching up twenty feet and a monster woodstove tucked in a fieldstone chimney. "How come no open fireplace?" I asked. Would have looked better with the log walls.

"Have you ever been in minus forty? All the heat gets sucked up the chimney." She turned. "God, I need a drink. Or five."

There was a box of kindling and newspaper along with the maple and birch splits. I got a roaring blaze fired up. Some of the chimney rocks had gold and silver glints.

Gladys appeared in the doorway with a full glass in her hand.

"Nice going. I turned on the hot-water heater for morning. Now come to bed and warm my toes."

"Yes, m...I mean Gladdie." I tried to smile. She'd worn me out again last night. I wasn't anywhere near her toes.

"Sweet. George never was one for nicknames." She assessed me with a turn of her head. "The sheets are musty. I'll be ordering fresh linen this week."

The next morning I awoke under a big red blanket. Hudson's Bay, she said. At first I thought I was in a hotel. Then I remembered. My nose prickled. Pancakes?

I got up and pulled on the new jeans and tucked in the pearl-buttoned shirt. A pair of sheepskin slippers was laid out for me. Bucky was still asleep in a big armchair in the corner.

The master suite, twenty by twenty, had log walls varnished to a shine. There was matching furniture with chests of drawers, a tall cabinet and a makeup table for Gladys. On top of a desk was a silver-framed portrait of a guy with thick white hair. Guess who? Seventies clothes and that mullet cut. Then a marriage shot of them somewhere with blue water and palms. Hawaii? George reminded me of my dad. That gave me a shiver. In the walk-in closet, one side held her clothes, the other his. I touched a charcoal suit. Custom-made in Toronto. Drawers of sweaters and rows of monogrammed shirts. Funny thing was, I was just his size, down to the shoes.

"George, old man, I think I'm going to like it here," I said.

In the large marble bathroom, Gladys had laid out a shaving set. A bristle brush and a tube of some fancy cream. A razor and some Old Spice. I jumped into the weird shower. Controls, hoses and nozzles everywhere. I combed my hair and brushed my teeth. Clicked them together in the mirror. Even blew myself a kiss.

"Come and get it, cowboy," she called from below. A triangle dinged. Something she used for the guests. I felt like a movie star.

I passed several bedrooms. Gladys had said that the overflow from the cabins sometimes stayed here. At higher rates, of course.

In the kitchen she was loading a platter with eggs, sausages, pancakes and baked beans. "I keep my men well fed, Rick." I dug in and noticed that she helped herself to a full plate.

It was good, I told her. When I finished, I lit a cigarette. Gladys cleared the table.

"Any gold or silver mining up here? Saw those glints in the rocks in the fireplace."

One corner of her mouth turned up.

"That's fool's gold. The tourists always try to pick it out with knives. Poor jerks. Adds to the atmosphere though."

She was looking at her watch and frowning. I pushed back my chair.

"Come on outside," she said. "There's work to be done. We're going to need three new cabins."

Now the idea hit me. She never exactly said I'd get any help, but...

"Three? How can—?"

She tossed an arm around my shoulders. "Sleeping cabins only. Simple framing and plywood sheets. Post and beam. No foundations needed. No running water or bathrooms either. Part of the charm. We can do the electric. You'll be fine. George built our main lodge almost all by himself."

Not in a few months, I thought, scratching a lump on my ear. The first bug had awakened. Must have come out of the woodpile by the stove once things warmed up.

Behind the lodge, she pointed at a grove of mature cedars.

"Gas up the chainsaw. Cut down that stuff. Put it in twelve-foot lengths. We'll have it milled next week and kiln dried. They can send out a skidder and a log truck. I'm not paying for wood when we have our own source."

I worked until lunch. Only May and three bites already. Might have been the aftershave.

Finally she came out with a platter of sandwiches and some pop. "No beer?" I was bone tired. I'd rather have been riding Nufflo. Clean horse sweat and saddle leather.

"No more than a six-pack a day. I don't want you to cut your pretty head off with that saw." She mimed a chainsaw bucking over her back. Guy I knew went that way.

I cleared the lot by five. Someone with a backhoe would have to take the stumps. When I stopped the saw to add oil, a neighbor with silver hair got out of a Jeep and came over to admire the piles of logs. Over a heavy shirt and cords, he wore a fishing vest with a million pockets. "So you're the new man. Looks like Gladys found herself a young one," the guy said. His name was Harvey.

"I'm the foreman. Rick Cooper." I almost didn't offer my hand. No use making enemies.

"Sure you are, pal. And more power to you." He made a broad gesture. "Leastways something's happening again. She was hitting the bottle pretty hard after George died, poor little girl. Guess you're the answer to a maiden's prayer."

"Listen here," I said. I stabbed a finger at his nose. "You're a friend of Gladdie. I'll forget about your bad manners."

* * *

In the next few weeks she sent me out on the property on the quad. It was rough country. A thin layer of peaty soil over the Cambrian rock shield. Enough hills to make it tricky. A hundred lakes in a hundred miles. Good for moose and bear though. There were places no one had ever been. Even in the winter with a snow-mobile, you couldn't get into some spots.

Gladys told me how things worked. Counting the new ones, she'd have six cabins with double beds. Meals came with the plan. She made even more on liquor. There wasn't any option out here, two hours from Elliot Lake.

Gladys told me that before George died, they cleared eighty thousand a year. That included the spring bear hunt. We were too late for that.

"Damn government in Toronto's talking about canceling the spring hunt. Wusses. Us lodge owners oughta have as many rights as animals. How are we supposed to make a living?"

"Know what you mean. They're always trying to call the shots for us in Salt Lake City."

She shrugged. "Men have to hunt. That's their nature. If we do well this fall, we'll be back in business big-time. I'm placing ads in three outdoor magazines. That's gonna cost, but it'll bring the bucks."

I cleared my throat. "When's payday?" I asked. My first month was nearly up.

She gave me a steely look. "This is a seasonal job. When I start getting money, you will too." Then she reached for her purse on the table. "Here's fifty. Don't know what you need it for. Everything's provided. Nothing to spend it on anyway."

She seemed to know her business. I'd hang around for the time being. When that money came in, I'd get my share. She was giving Bucky another Milk-Bone when I went up to bed.

CHAPTER FIVE

By mid-July the cabins were nearly finished. I sat on the front porch before supper, cleaning and oiling a twelve gauge. It had a carved stock. Nice piece.

"Where'd you get that?" Gladys asked. One dark eyebrow arched into a question.

"In the gun case in the den. It wasn't locked."

She gave me a funny look.

"That's George's best gun. I..." She paused and looked out across the woods. "Mind you take care of it."

"Damn straight. I'm going after a few birds tomorrow," I said. "I got the shingles on the new cabins. Tight as a tick. We're nearly good to go." Did she expect me to work seven days a week?

She nodded. "I suppose you earned a day off. Take Buck with you. He loves to hunt. Bit of a lard ass lately with all this winter rest. That's bad for his arthritis."

The ancient animal lay on the porch, tail switching at flies. Nothing made him move fast. Not since that first time we arrived. I was no babysitter.

"Are you kidding? That dog won't hunt."

She narrowed her eyes. "He was George's pal. You should have seen him in his youth. A soft mouth. Never put tooth on a partridge or a duck. That's a thousand-dollar dog."

"Maybe so. But he's stiffer than hell. Can't hardly get up some mornings."

Her voice took on an edge. "You'll be old like him someday, Rick. If you're lucky."

The next morning, Bucky ambled after me sort of senile-like. I let him come as far as the creek, then told him to go lay down. He stood there, that sappy golden retriever smile on his face. Not even enough brains to take offense. Then he circled twice and flopped down under a spreading maple.

Half an hour later, on an old path in the thick cedars, I leaned on a big-daddy yellow birch. Good hunters were patient. I enjoyed the clear air and the stuttery motoring of a ruffed grouse looking for a mate. Something caught my eye in the next spruce. I aimed up, slowly, ready to lead it if it moved. Then I fired. Got the head clean off. No shot in my meat.

And I got four more soon after that. All in all a good hunt. And they were fat too. I stood on the wings and pulled the feet. The skin came off and the gut bag with it.

Good as chicken any day. When I got back to the creek, Bucky raised his head at the smell of the birds in my bag.

"Want to grab one now, don't you, old bugger?" I said and shoved him aside with my leg. That same loopy smile followed me.

I brought the birds into the kitchen.

"Not bad, mighty hunter," Gladys said, topping up her drink. "I'm making fried potatoes and grouse fingers. Bucky gets a share too."

I started laughing as I popped a beer.

"I told you that dog won't hunt. He slept the whole time."

Her face got hard and her chin stuck out.

"That's not the point. Take him out with you when you go. I mean it, Rick."

I kept quiet. What she didn't know wouldn't hurt her.

A week later, Gladys called me over to one of the cabins. I was finishing the drywall, hustling around those big sheets. Cheaper in twelve-foot lengths but a bitch to move. My face was covered with dust and sweat.

"I need a Shop-Vac from the hardware. This stuff will blow your canister set all to hell."

"All right. Get one." She held a level on the framing. The bubble dipped up same as my Adam's apple. "These lines aren't true. Measure twice, cut once."

I hadn't stopped since seven. It was nearly dinnertime.

"Oh hell, it's good enough. Let it settle a bit. What do you think this is? Palm Springs?" I had a drywall knife in my hand. With the other, I wormed a blackfly from my ear. The bloody crust came away. Sneaky. I hate them worst.

"I have pride in my place. George wouldn't have paid you. A good workman is worth his hire." She folded her arms.

"A workman? Thought I was more than that to you." I scuffed a piece of drywall across the floor. "So get me some more help. Even a gofer. A kid would do."

She turned those cold blue eyes on me. Like a little robot.

"I picked you up on the road, bud. You owe me."

The money was coming. I couldn't bail out now.

"Sorry, babe. I'm just tired." I hung my head like a good boy and waited.

Her voice softened. "Take the weekend off. Harvey brought over some moose steaks. You have been working pretty hard. And guess what?" She pulled a paper from her jacket pocket. "I have bookings for four straight weeks already. What do you know about taking people on a bear hunt?"

I shrugged. "Hunting is hunting, I guess."

"George used to hire a man from Chapleau, but now you're it. I've ordered

some new equipment from Cabela's."
She pulled out a catalog and thumbed it.
"These new tree perches are way more
comfortable for our soft city friends. You'll
be replacing the old wood ones. And there's
a game trike too. Saves on manpower."

"I better get back to work, Gladys."

Omitting her pet name struck a blow.

"I do have expenses, you know. I'm still
paying off a loan when they brought in the
hydro from the main road. I can give you
a couple hundred next week. But what the
hell you need it for out here, I haven't a
clue," she said as she walked out.

A couple of days later Gladys was
napping on the couch after dinner. She'd be
good until the late news started. Time to
find out exactly where I stood. She kept the
accounts in her little office. I stood near her
and clapped my hands. Nada. Out like a light.

I turned the TV off so's I could hear if
she got up. Then I went around upstairs to

her office. Those wooden stairs were fierce for a creak. I started with the files. It was pretty clear that she hadn't done any business in the last five years. Then I tackled the checkbook and a couple of bankbooks. Finances don't mean much to me, but I knew enough to see that she had a potful. I sat down and felt my fists bunch up. Then a dark haze came over my eyes. I shook myself and pounded a fist into my palm. Cool off, boy.

Couldn't touch anything in the bank, that's for sure. For a crazy minute I wondered if she would marry me. All's I had to do was pretend I didn't know about this. Turn up the sweetness machine. What's that thing called community property? My head started to ache. The humid climate was doing a number on me.

CHAPTER SIX

The first of August Gladys sent me to Elliot Lake to buy some paint. The place was almost ready for our visitors. "First impressions are important for return trade," she said. "Word-of-mouth is critical. These business guys have a network you wouldn't believe. And take Bucky with you. George always did. Put him in the cab, not the truck bed. And you might give him a brush sometime to keep down the dog hair."

With the dog padding after me, I went to the shed for the old GMC pickup.

Next to a 50cc kiddie motorcycle and a riding mower was the Mustang in all its candy-apple glory. "Sure wish you and me was driving down a desert highway, sweetheart," I said, rubbing off some dust. It hadn't left the building since we returned. What a waste of muscle. Not that there was anywhere to drive to up here.

As I chugged the two hours to town, Bucky stinking like a dozen rotten eggs, I took stock. I saved everything she'd given me, but all I had was five hundred dollars in a bag in a drawer. And some small change in my jeans. Everything at the hardware was charged. No way to fudge on that.

At the cash, where I made my order, the most beautiful babe in the world gave me a twenty-carat smile. I was always a sucker for curly red hair. Means there's fire inside. Her green eyes were sparkly and welcoming. I was glad I had shaved that morning.

"Hello, there," she said. "I've seen you before. Got a big project, eh?"

We passed the time of day. Place was kind of empty. Under her smock, I could see her flat tummy. Legs to heaven and back. No ring. Women usually wore them. With working men, they got in the way. For a lot of reasons.

"What's to do around this here town?" I asked. Gladys had started drinking at noon. Something about George's birthday. If she asked me what took so long, I'd say I had a flat tire.

Shelley said she was getting off at three, so we made a date.

"Ever been to LA?" I asked. "Just got back myself."

A dimple opened on one cheek. "Gosh, I haven't even been across the border. What's it like out west? I thought I heard something in your voice. You don't sound like you're from around here." She looked at me like I was ten feet tall. I felt my chest get bigger.

We met at the Dairy Queen down the block. I'd let the air mostly out of one tire and taken the truck to a service station. The receipt made a good excuse. Bucky was still snoring in the cab.

Shelley ordered a Peanut Buster Parfait, and I had a Blizzard with Skor-bar pieces. We talked about our favorite old music. We both liked the B-52's. Jon Bon Jovi was Shelley's heartthrob.

"You look like Charlie Sheen." Her eyes were clear and flirty. "He was so cute in *Young Guns*."

"You can take the cowboy out of the West, but you can't—"

We completed the sentence at the same time. I almost laughed, but she put out her little pinky and linked mine. I felt a familiar flicker.

"Did you make a wish?" she asked.

I caught on to the game and nodded. If she read minds, she'd know.

"How about you, Shelley? Got a boyfriend, I bet. Gal as pretty as you."

She waved her hand. "They're all just silly boys around here. Sweet, but real losers."

Then she told me about her family, who had moved to Calgary when her father was laid off from the mill. She was living with an aunt.

"I just stayed to finish high school. Soon as I save up some money I'm going to Calgary. Or maybe Vancouver. I don't know. Anywhere out of here."

"I hear you," I said. "Too many mosquitoes too. Give me the wide-open spaces." I described to her that little spread I'd seen near Big Water.

"Is it near Vegas? I've always wanted to see a show," she said. "My aunt saw Dolly Parton there."

I waved a hand. "Right next door. Best of all worlds."

She sighed and leaned forward. Her plump red lips sucked on the spoon. "Sounds like a dream."

After that, Shelley and I met whenever I was in town for supplies.

"I'm planning on leaving here soon as the hunting's over," I said over lunch at Micky D's.

"That's what I thought. Bet Mrs. Ryan will be sorry to see you go," Shelley said. She gave my biceps a little squeeze, and I firmed 'em up. "She probably has a crush on you."

"Gladys can be a mite jealous. You know older women," I said, tracing my fingers on her hand. So smooth and supple. She always smelled clean and pure, like baby powder. I wanted to put my arms around her, the way she looked up at me. "Firecracker," I called her.

"She's old for sure," Shelley said. "I used to see her in here with George when I was a kid. The B word. Thinks she knows it all."

A pretty pulse throbbed in that soft part in her throat.

CHAPTER SEVEN

A week later the cabins were done. Couldn't have been soon enough for me, hauling in that new furniture. It was time to get the bear-baiting sites ready.

"In five years, the trails have overgrown. Brush hook's in the shed. That's all you'll need for saplings," she said. "Start tomorrow. Take one of the quads. The tree perches arrived, so don't forget them. Make sure you have all your tools. It's a long way out."

Then she got out a topo map. "Look here."

Her finger stabbed on ten places. Then she made circles with a pen. "First, we'll bait the area. Stale baked goods work best. Some people pour used fry oil on logs. That gets their noses working great. But you can't get rid of it. We don't want them still around in moose season."

"This is a big territory." I thought about the hours this would take.

"Over four-hundred-square miles, including the Crown land. That's a minimum. But we use it. We'll have more than one party in the field at once. Some hunt with fiber bows or crossbows. And you know how far a slug carries. They need that separation."

"I'm a cowboy not a hunter. What do people want with bears anyway? Their meat's not prime like a deer or moose."

"It's big game to these slickers. They take the skins. Sometimes the natives make sausage and roasts for those who can take it home with dry ice. Others leave the carcass. We haul it to the dump. Disgusts me, to tell you the truth. Ever seen a stripped bear?"

"Not in Utah."

"It looks human." She shuddered. "Not that I've seen many humans without skin. Except in horror movies."

She sipped at her coffee, "sweetened" with a splash of Seagram's. Coffee royale, she called it. One excuse for drinking at ten in the morning. Makes a wide-awake drunk.

"We'll start our baits well before the hunters arrive. Refresh as necessary. That will get the bears coming while they're putting on their final layer of fat. The coats look like shit in April."

"How long is the season?" I leaned forward, checking out the contour lines to gauge the best paths.

"First three weeks of September. That's why I was cracking the whip. We can push it a day or two out here. But that's our best time. Our success rate used to be over eighty percent. And with five years of no hunters..." She mocked a pistol shot and blew on her finger.

"How many...clients do you get?"

"Ten to twelve a week booked up. Remember what they're paying."

Math wasn't my strong point. "Say an even ten times...that's big money." I gave a low whistle.

She fooled with my hair. "You're no businessman. That's not all profit. We have the gear, food, gas for the quads, and the hired help. I'm going to need someone to serve. You might have to fill in once or twice. Young girls aren't that reliable."

I had thought of myself going from table to table, brew in my hand, talking up the Yanks. Not like some freakin' waiter. "Oh, sure."

"On a normal day, here's the routine. Bait sites checked at dawn. Then around two, after we get a big meal into them, you run the hunters out to the stands."

"Didn't you say ten or more? Every damn day? That's going to take hours."

She gave a rough laugh that set my teeth on edge. "I know men. Some will go out once, then sit around and drink. Fall asleep braced up in a tree. Roughing it in the bush. That's what they're out here for."

"Where do these idjits come from?"

"Believe it or not, we do real well with Iowa. All that corn and nothing to do till shucking time, I guess. Quite a few from Georgia too. And the big cities like Chicago and Detroit."

"Why go out so late in the day?"

"Half of them are hungover until noon. Prime time for bears is late afternoon until dark. Anyway, the men will be picked up shortly after sunset, so you'd better know where the hell you're going. And log out and in using our site numbers. I need to know where you are."

Cell phones didn't work out here, nor did walkie-talkies.

I was getting bored with all this info. Did she think I was stupid? "Anything else, boss?"

"They'll be generous with tips when they get a kill. And take their pictures with that camera in the office. They love that."

That tips part sounded good.

"Then we have to go back for the meat?"

"There's a small trailer for that. One of the locals will take care of the skinning and keep the meat. We serve it sometimes. Authentic. It's really kind of sweet. George knew all the right spices."

I wanted to see light at the end of the tunnel. Shelley and me snuggling as we watched the sun shimmer down behind the mountains in our little place in Utah.

"When's moose season start?"

"Right after bear. Five weeks ending in the middle of November. During the rut."

From a nail on the wall, she pulled off a birch-bark cone. "Home made. They love it."

She made it wail like she was playing a sax. "Practice up. You can also take a bucket of water."

"For drinking? That doesn't make—"

She rolled those cruel ocean eyes. The red veins were making them nearly pink.

"To imitate a cow pissing. The males hear it for miles."

"No shit." I couldn't believe these guys made such fools of themselves.

"Another thing. With moose, there's less guarantee of a kill. Fewer animals is why. People could wait ten years to get a tag. That's why they come to us. We leave the men off for the day in groups of three.

Make sure they're at opposite ends of our preserve."

I cleared my throat. "Do they all pay in advance?"

"You *are* turning into a businessman. I'm not sure I like that." She cocked her head and looked at me a little squinty-eyed. "Of course they make a down payment. The rest when they arrive. If we do well, there's a bonus for you."

"So you're talking…" I let my voice trail off. She didn't look liked she trusted me anymore.

"I told you. A fair share." She raised her cup and toasted me. "Here's to us."

She gave what passed for a smile, then drained the mug. The smell of hot rye made my stomach turn. "Get on into town to advertise for kitchen help. Put this up on the bulletin boards all over." She handed me ten copies of what she'd written on the computer. Hardly more than minimum wage.

But they got tips too. Like me. On the way outside, I nearly tripped over Bucky. Damn dog was always in the way. And that hair. My clothes were full of it.

CHAPTER EIGHT

September first, the place was jumping. Sixteen-hour days for me. I was busy taking guys out, bringing them back. I lost count of the stinking bears. Killing twenty wouldn't even make a dent in their numbers. And that bear stew? Nearly made me hurl.

Gladys had hired two girls, one to help in the kitchen and the other to serve and clean. They were both eighteen but hardly jail bait. One had zits like a lunar landscape; the other was a cow. My boss could be found noon to midnight drinking with the clients. The old farts seemed to like her. They were happy to leave their wives behind and listen to her hunting stories.

An Ojibway guy came over when a bear was shot. Didn't talk much but he knew his stuff. One morning Gladys called to me. "Get rid of that carcass in the shed. The landfill is closed this week. That's what we do with the extras."

"What do you mean by 'get rid'? Bury it?" That would be no picnic. The soil was only thin peat over boulders.

"Don't be stupid. Take it a couple miles out and dump it. It won't be around long with the brush wolves that I've heard howling. Bruno will be riding in the belly of the beast by midnight. Think of it like a soup kitchen for animals."

"Where exactly? We don't want to be near the hunting spots."

"Do I have to think for you? Try over by Kinsol Mountain." She pointed on the map.

"Nobody goes there. Don't leave it anywhere near the trails."

"This isn't that big boar, is it?" My muscles were aching from the day-to-dusk activity. She had me splitting some damn stubborn birch this morning.

"A two-year-old cub the guy carried in himself. Idiot said he thought it was a deer. He's keeping the pelt for a rug anyway." She shook her head in disgust. You weren't supposed to kill sows or cubs, but hunters often made "a mistake."

Inside the shed, Bucky was sniffing at the body. Looked like a young kid without the fur. Flies had already found it.

"Get out of there, you good-for-nothing hound," I said, giving him a little poke with my foot. He grunted, but I could tell I hadn't hurt him none. Bucky was so deaf, wasn't much sense yelling at him.

Then I wrapped the carcass in a tarp and tossed it over the quad carrier. In an hour,

I was deep in the forest, at the bottom of Kinsol. Leaving the quad, I doubled the tarp over the body and pulled it up the mountain. Every ten minutes I'd stop to rest. Finally past the roughest terrain, I saw a deep cleft between rock ledges. No path went within miles of here. I pulled the body to the edge, then shifted it down. It fell about thirty feet into a dark, cavernous spot, the mouth of hell. Then I pushed over some hundred-pound rocks for cover.

"Rest in peace, cubby," I said. "Plenty more bears where you came from." Blood and gore covered my flannel shirt and work pants. I couldn't stand to smell myself.

When I got back, Gladys called me over. "I need you to help serve. The girls couldn't make it tonight. Thank god there are leftovers." Her nose gave a sniff. "For Christ's sake, clean up first. And clean up good."

I was dog tired. "I need half an hour."

"You've got half of that. There's a fifty in it for you." Her head moved around at a roar of happy men in the great room. Glasses and bottles were clinking. Frank Sinatra was on the stereo singing "My Way."

Eight men sat on leather sofas and chairs in front of the woodstove. The projection-screen TV pulled in over two hundred channels on satellite. They were watching a football game, eating popcorn and drinking rye with beer chasers at double the going rate. "Jesus, what's that reek? Somebody die?" one of them asked.

By eleven, the men had taken the party to their cabins. House rules. Gladys was snoring on the couch. I played with the remote until it brought up a movie. Black and white. A golden oldie. It starred this James Dean guy with hair like Elvis. I was about to turn it off when a scene interested me. Dad had told me about this once. The game was called Chickie Run. You raced your old cars, Dad called them jalopies, toward a cliff. First one to jump out was a chicken and the loser. Even though my eyelids were heavy, I couldn't turn it off. Right at the edge, one smart guy jumped and rolled, and the other dude got his sleeve caught on the door handle. He went over the cliff. The dead guy won. Some joke.

* * *

Then moose season started. Less driving around for me, since the hunters were out all day as a group. But moose were way more dangerous than bears. One wild bull came at me one afternoon by a swamp, and I barely made it up a tree. Maybe they just wanted their women, but they were plain nuts.

I noticed that Gladys took American cash on the barrelhead. No checks. No charge cards.

"Damn government wants my blood for taxes," she said. "I'll declare half. 'Taxed to the max' is not my motto. Ottawa doesn't care about us Northerners anyhow."

"What about my share?" I spoke up more loudly than usual. There was only a week of hunting to go. For what she was "giving" me, plus the bedtime services, it worked out to five bucks an hour.

"I've got your money for you, Rick," she said with an irritated sigh. "Look how you pissed so much away in that poker game with that Chicago guy the other night. When we settle up, you can head south again. But there's always a place for you here once the season starts. Now that we're open again, we'll start in the spring." She was wrapping up hundreds with a rubber band. Her sharp look told me to clear off.

On her desk was a metal box.

One morning before she got up, I tried the file cabinet in her office. Not even locked. Nothing but records anyway. Where was her hidey-hole? A day later I found the loose board in the floor of the bedroom closet. Piles and piles of hundred-dollar bills. I was counting it when I heard the stairs squeak. I knew where it was. She didn't know I knew. That was my advantage.

CHAPTER NINE

On November 16, Gladys and I waved goodbye to the last American rolling out of the drive in a Lincoln Town Car. She looked at me and folded her arms like she was satisfied.

"I thawed some steaks. Let's you and me celebrate."

"Just as long as it's beef."

"Triple-A Alberta prime."

In three hours, four bottles of wine lined up like dead soldiers. Half a bottle of cognac. We were lying on the big leather reclining sofa. "So this is it. I'm out of here before the snow flies. That desert's calling me."

A slump passed over her face. Maybe she would miss me.

"Sure you won't change your mind and come along? I always travel over the winter. Hot places. Southern California. Vegas. Even your precious Utah if you like. We'll have lots of referrals now. Then with a better year—"

"I don't think so." Something hit me as strange. "So we'll be settling up tomorrow, right? But what do you mean *better*? Didn't we do good?" She had told me that she turned away at least three parties. We were full up every night.

She lit a cigarette and puffed a little white cloud. Tapped it into an ashtray.

"Not...quite as good as I thought. Remember those renovations. And I'm still paying off the loan George took to bring the hydro lines in. I figure your cut is about six.

There's a check for you in my office. After all, it's my place. And you got room and board. Like in a quality hotel."

Hotel my ass. Labor camp more like.

"I don't care none about what you and damn George did. I worked my guts out for you. A deal's a deal."

The room turned to red mist. A vice squeezed my head as if my eyes were gonna pop like marbles. I couldn't catch my breath.

"If that's the way you feel, I can make it six and a half. No hard feelings."

Steam was coming out my ears, but Gladys didn't even seem to notice. She swirled the cognac in that big fat glass. Her mouth opened like a shark. The lipstick was sucked back in little creases. I picked up the last bottle and chugged it, then smashed it against the wall.

"You'll clean that up, buddy boy. The help's all gone. What a waste of good liquor. It's better bred than you are."

She said something else that made her laugh. Blah, blah, blah, Rick. My ears were roaring like a jet on takeoff. I think I grabbed her arm, and we both shoved. Then she slapped me and that ring cut my temple. She staggered back, screamed and came at me, butting into my chest. I gave her a pop to the jaw.

Next thing I knew Gladys was lying with her head at a funny angle by the fireplace. That shiny gold rock. No blood. At first I thought maybe she wasn't hurt bad. Just knocked out. The heat from the fire was burning my face. But the rest of me was stone cold. Then I noticed that her eyes were open. Those ugly blue cesspools seeing through to nothing. I checked. No pulse. Even if I knew CPR, I wasn't about to bring the old bitch back. Shit, I wasn't even sorry. She'd worked me like a slave.

I grabbed a bottle of rye and sat back down on the sofa. The booze went down like water. My thoughts lined up like those grouse in a tree. One, two, three. Shoot.

The alcohol worked its magic, and my breathing finally slowed. I thought about the situation. It started not to look so bad. Gladys had paid everyone off. She was expected to head south at this time. The lodge would soon close like it did every year.

It was so quiet that I could hear my heart beat. The big grandfather clock in the corner struck. I jumped like a frightened cat.

Time was on my side if I didn't panic. I bundled Gladys up in a sheet and put her in the laundry room. Funny that I hadn't seen Bucky. He seemed to be losing it these days. Standing around, staring at nothing. I left a pan of old rice on the porch. Then I turned in.

I hadn't been asleep long when a nightmare startled me awake. I was running down Smoky Mountain Road outside of Escalante. Gladys was chasing me with the Mach 1. Its grill was opened like a cottonmouth, ready to swallow me. I could feel its hot breath.

It was some time before I drifted off again. Next thing I knew, the sun was coming through the window. I half expected Gladys to be calling me for breakfast. Downstairs all was quiet. I went out for a smoke. Still no sign of Bucky. A pile of ants ran around the untouched rice.

My appetite wasn't much. I gulped down two cups of coffee strong enough to remove shingles. Then I took Gladys to the shed. I roped her onto the back of our biggest quad and set off.

"You're gonna see someplace where the hand of man has never set foot." That made me laugh. Count on me never to lose my sense of humor.

It took an hour to get back to the deepest part of the forest around Kinsol Mountain. Then I set off on foot. Neat and clean.

No tracks. With the ground hard, the going was easier than usual. Snow was predicted for tomorrow night.

Gladys weighed about a hundred pounds. More than the cub. My muscles were shrieking as it got steeper. Fir, spruce, pesky alder raked at me. Nothing but a moose would come here, or something with jaws and claws. There was that cleft, the baby bear's tomb. No sign of it down in those dark shadows.

"You should have played fair with me, Gladdie."

Off she went. That hand mocked me, sticking out with the ring. I tossed down some rocks and moss until it was covered.

* * *

That night as I finished the last of the rye, I thought about the plan. She'd been telling everyone that she was leaving for the Southwest as usual. Then I stopped and hit myself upside the head. One problem, fool. Why's the Mustang still in the shed? No wonder I had dreamed about it. Pay attention! It's only been one day. You have time.

Gladys had a forever home. Now the car needed one. Consulting the topos, I found the deepest lake in the vicinity. A meteor crater, some said. Over six hundred feet in the middle. An old logging road ran nearby along a steep cliff. The Mustang had low clearance, but if I pushed her, she'd make it. That car had guts to spare.

I left at night just in case anyone might be on the highway. The little 50cc motorbike was in the trunk. At the site, I slept in the car. When dawn came, I stood at the side of the road looking down about sixty feet. I picked up a large rock and pitched it. *Splash!* Into that blue water until you couldn't see it anymore. *Rebel Without a Cause*, that's me. Except that I had a good one. Too bad about the car. She was prime.

I hauled the little motorcycle out of the trunk.

"Goodbye, old friend," I said as I fired up the Mustang. I aimed her for the lip of the canyon. It wasn't in the cards for us to stay together. I had the door open and my left foot ready to hit the ground. I gunned her and pitched out plenty early, rolling in the gravel. I skinned my elbow pretty good and tore the sleeve of my jacket. I'd have a damn good bruise on my hip, but nothing was broken. My luck was holding.

I almost cried when that cherry-red beauty disappeared under the water. With the windows wide-open, it went down real fast. Bubbles came up. Then all was still. An owl called. "I kno-o-o-ow. I kno-o-o-ow." Revving up the cycle, I rode the hydro-pole line back to where it crossed one corner of our property.

Just as I got back, it started to snow big time. That would put a nice blanket on everything, including the car tracks at the lake. Not that anyone ever went there.

I slept ten hours and got up feeling like a new man.

Then, on his next delivery, I told the postman about Gladys leaving for a few months as usual. Gave him the fee to hold her mail at the post office for six months.

I bided my sweet time, following every part of my plan. Shelley stayed with me one night at the lodge. She brought a pan of frozen cabbage rolls and a loaf of Wonder bread. With her looks, she didn't need to cook.

"Wow! Real French wine," she said when I hauled out the last bottle. It didn't cost but seven dollars.

"Nothing but the best for you, hon."

"Super nice," Shelley said. We were nestling in one of the corner bedrooms. It would have been a bit nervy to take the master. "This is all, like, so perfect, Rick.

With what I've saved and your job this summer, we'll get that place you told me about. Soon as I get packed in a few days, we can leave. My Toyota's ten years old, but it's in good shape."

From outside the window we could hear the wind shrieking as a front moved in. A major thaw was on the way, weatherman said.

"I can't wait to get away from all this snow."

"There's just enough in Utah to make the desert pretty," I said. "A little stardust." I covered her shoulder with butterfly kisses.

"How long will it take to get there?" she asked.

"We'll take our time and see the sights," I said. "Have some fun at the casinos in Michigan."

"And Vegas too?"

"Guaranteed." My finger tapped the tip of her tiny nose. "Five or six times a year."

"Tell me about your ranch, Rick," she asked.

"*Our* ranch. I'll put up a real fancy sign. The R Circle S." I drew her a brand in the air. The radio was playing "Something Happened on the Way to Heaven." I couldn't help but smile.

"What's so funny?" She licked her bottom lip like she wanted to understand the joke.

"Nothing, babe." I could drown in those emerald eyes. Little flecks of gold I never noticed. "Let's take a bubble bath."

"You're so romantic." We got out of bed. Then she stepped on the Mr. Chile dog toy. It squeaked. "So what happened to Bucky? Did Mrs. Ryan take him?"

For once I didn't feel like lying.

"That's the funny thing. He wandered off just before she left. She'd arranged for Harvey to take care of him anyway. Figured he was getting too old for the heat down south."

"Yeah, he's pretty old. I guess he's had a good life."

"Gladys has a soft heart. If he can walk and still enjoys his food, his ticket won't be punched. But suffering, that's another story. She left Harvey the name of her vet in case."

"My mom said that dogs are our best friends."

"You got it."

Flea factory. And let's not forget the shit I stepped in when he took a dump too close to the house. And that had gotten more and more often. Lazy bastard.

I biffed Mr. Chile into the toybox.

CHAPTER TEN

Time to go. Gladys, check. Car, check. Money, check. Shelley was picking me up at noon.

The money was all in those nice American hundreds plus some traveling Canadian cash. Fast as a bug, we'd disappear into red-rock country. As for Gladys, when she didn't return in the spring, what the hell could anyone do? People went missing all the time in the US. Even in Canada. Even with their cars. And there was no way anyone was heading anywhere near Kinsol Mountain. Not until 2190 when they built a Walmart.

That morning the thaw arrived. Ten degrees above freezing was sending the early snow packing. The eaves were dripping with icicles. I was having a last coffee on the porch, enjoying the warm wind, when Harvey came along. I'd forgotten to tell him about Bucky's wanderings. Luck was being a lady to me.

He rolled up the drive in his Jeep, skewing in the slush.

"Crazy weather, or what?" he said, taking off a tweedy wool hat as he got out. "Not that I'm complaining."

"Come on up to the porch. Coffee's hot."

Giving me a friendly grin, he took a rocker. I brought out the coffee and gave him the mug. He cradled it in his hands and sipped.

"Haven't seen a thaw this early since 1975. It's pneumonia weather," he said.

"Damn straight. I think I'm getting a cold." I cleared my throat for effect.

"How's Gladys doing?" he asked. "She get there yet?"

My heart thumped a beat.

"She called the other day. Her arthritis is a lot better down in Southern California."

"That's what she always says. Too bad she can't live there. No health care though. So what are your plans?" he asked, looking around. "See you got the shutters locked and the place all secured."

"I'm going today when my...ride comes. But I might be back in the spring." Leaving a door open was a good idea to take the heat off me. "She said to tell you to keep the drive free." I reached for my wallet and peeled off two hundred dollars.

With a grin, he pocketed the money.

"Hey, I ain't seen old Buck come around in a while," he said, sipping the coffee. Harvey kept steak bones for him.

I raised an eyebrow.

"I'm worried too. Seems he went off...a few days ago. I was thinking a coyote or wolf got him. Easy pickings. I've seen their tracks in the snow. Keep an eye out. Gladys will settle up for his care. And you know the vet she uses." Only one in town.

Harvey nodded, and I was congratulating myself on the story. Had I covered all the bases or what? Ten days tops, and Nufflo would be nuzzling one cheek and Shelley the other.

"Poor schnook," he said, rubbing his knee. "He was a heck of a dog when he was young though. George hunted him from the time he was a pup."

I folded my arms and chuckled.

"Come on, now. That dog won't hunt."

"You didn't know him when. Nose like a bloodhound. What a birder. George never went out but he came back loaded. Ducks in the fall, grouse and partridge all winter."

Both our mugs were empty. I should offer a refill, but I wanted him on his way. Instead of joining into the conversation, I just ummed a bit.

"Hey, isn't that Buck?" Harvey asked as a honey-colored form appeared from back of the shed. "Holy jumpin'. Didn't I tell you? What's that in his mouth? Get you a bunny, Mr. Buck?"

We both stood as the dog limped slowly forward. Its fur was matted and tufted. One ear was half torn off. Blood streamed from his nose.

"He's in a bad way. Come, boy." Harvey got up and extended a hand.

At the bottom of the porch, Bucky stopped and dropped the five-fingered burden.

"That's no rabbit," Harvey said as he turned to me, his eyes narrowing.

That cigar-band ring was lucky one last time.

LOU ALLIN is the author of the Belle Palmer Mystery series set in Northern Ontario. Now living on Vancouver Island with her border collies and mini-poodle, she is working on a new series where the rainforest meets the sea. *That Dog Won't Hunt* is her first title in the new Rapid Reads series from Orca's Raven Books imprint.

RAPID READS

The following is an excerpt from
another exciting Rapid Reads novel,
The Way It Works by William Kowalski.

978-1-55469-367-2 $9.95 pb

Can Walter Davis succeed when the odds are
stacked against him?

Walter Davis is young, handsome, intelligent and
personable. He is also homeless. The medical
expenses that came with his mother's unsuccessful
battle with cancer have left him destitute. When he
meets the girl of his dreams, his situation gets even
more complicated. Trying to impress a girlfriend
when you have no fixed address proves difficult.
And when he's caught in a lie, she shuns his company.
Only resilience, ingenuity and his drive to succeed
can bring Walter back from the brink of despair.

CHAPTER ONE

You probably think you can tell if someone is homeless just by looking at them. But you're wrong. You can't. Because not every homeless person looks like a bum. Take it from me. I'm an expert. Nothing in this world is as it seems.

Look at that guy over there. The one in the brown uniform, unloading boxes from the delivery truck. He looks clean. He has a job. Maybe not a great one, but it's a job. How much you think he makes? Minimum wage. Maybe a dollar more.

Well, you can't make it on minimum anymore. Not in this city.

So how does he get by? Maybe he lives with his parents. Maybe his wife has a job too. Or maybe he washed his face and hair in the bathroom of a McDonald's this morning. Maybe he sleeps in the back of his truck. You just don't know.

Here's another one. A well-dressed white lady, sitting on that bench over there. She's got a skirt suit and high heels on. There's a nice purse in her lap. She's all dainty, the way she eats out of that plastic container. Her pinky sticks out like she's at a tea party. You look at her and you think, *Rich*. Or at least comfortable.

But wait a minute. If she's so comfortable, why is she just sitting there on a bench downtown at nine thirty in the morning? Could be she's just killing time. Or maybe she has nowhere else to go. Maybe those clothes are the only nice things she owns.

Maybe she got that food out of a trash can, and she's trying to make it last, because she doesn't know where her next meal is coming from.

Or take this guy, now. A young, light-skinned black man. Maybe twenty-one, twenty-two years old, clean-cut, in good shape. Not a bad-looking guy. A little on the short side. He's wearing a beautiful suit and carrying a nice briefcase. His shoes are so shiny they hurt your eyes. He's bopping along the sidewalk like he owns the place. Full of self-confidence. A spring in his step. Looks like nothing can stop him. Like he's on his way to take over the world.

You would never know that this well-dressed young man slept in his car last night. Or that he can only afford to eat once a day. Or that he's been trying to get a job for the last six months, but no one will hire him.

How do I know all this?

Because that young black man is me.

I'm Walter Davis. I'm twenty years old. My moms and I moved to this city about a year ago. We didn't know anybody here. But there was lots of opportunity. Moms was already trained as a paralegal, and I was going to community college. This city was supposed to be a new start for us. A brand-new life. The beginning of something better.

And for a while, it was.

Things started out great. Moms got a job at an important law firm. She had to work hard, but the money was worth it. It was the first professional job she ever had. Before that, she was a waitress. This was a big step up.

We got an apartment in a decent part of the city. Not too much crime, no graffiti on the buildings. Little by little, we started getting all the things we dreamed of. Nice kitchen appliances. A set of furniture for the living room. A flat-screen TV. We even got a car. It was used, sure, but we didn't care. Our last car wasn't even from this century. Sometimes it didn't even work. Now we had a steel-gray 2000 Chevrolet Caprice. It ran like a dream.

We were coming up in the world.

For my twentieth birthday, right before I graduated, Moms gave me a present. It was a suit. But not just any suit. It was a pin-striped wool Turnbull & Asser. She also gave me a pair of Tanino Crisci shoes and an Underwood briefcase. It must have cost her thousands. I told her to take it all back. But she said she wanted me to look my best when I started going on job interviews. The world judges a man by how he looks, she said.

I don't think I ever saw my moms really happy until we moved here. And I was happy too. We had it rough for a long time. Happiness was a welcome change.

Then came the life-insurance exam.

Moms wanted some security for me, in case anything happened to her. She could get a good deal on a policy, but she had to go see a doctor first. No big deal, right?

Except the doctor found a spot on her lungs. "Oops," he said. "You better get that checked out."

So she did. There wasn't just one spot. There were more. It turned out to be advanced lung cancer. How did that happen? Moms didn't even smoke.

I'll make a long story short. I don't like feeling sorry for myself.

There was to be no life insurance. Soon, my moms was too sick to work. She lost her health insurance. I took care of her as best I could. She passed away in a public hospice, in a room full of other dying people. I was holding her hand.

At least I was there for her. Some folks in that place died alone.

I kept on trying to find a job. No one was interested. Times are tough.

Soon our building went co-op. I couldn't afford to buy in. They told me I had to leave.

I sold all the things we were so proud of: television, furniture, appliances. That gave me some cash. Not much though. Enough to get by for a couple of months.

I started looking for a new apartment. But guess what? Landlords don't want tenants who don't have a job. It's that simple. No job, no apartment. That's the way it works.

I moved the few things I still owned into the trunk of my car. The first night I had to sleep in the backseat, I vowed it would be the last.

But it wasn't.

Boom. Just like that, I was homeless.

It really is that easy to lose everything, all in the blink of an eye.